Whose Song Is It, Anyway?

The Mixed-Up Guitar Case

Two Sam Snow Mysteries

by Dina Anastasio
illustrated by Jennifer Morgan

Table of Contents

Mystery

What is a mystery?

A mystery is a story about a person solving a crime or uncovering the cause of a puzzling event. It is often solved by a professional detective, but the hero could be an amateur, for example, an elderly lady or a group of teenagers. The answer to the mystery is left unsettled until the end of the story.

What is the purpose of a mystery?

People often enjoy trying to figure out a mystery or a puzzle. Reading a mystery is an opportunity to follow the steps of a detective as he or she discovers clues. Part of the fun and challenge in reading mysteries is to match wits with the detective and solve the problem before he or she does. Mysteries are often entertaining for another reason: They are filled with suspense. The building action of a mystery makes the reader want to find out what happens next and eventually "who done it."

How do you read a mystery?

Pay close attention to the details. Something that seems unimportant may prove to be a key clue. A nervous smile or a single new nail in a board can turn out to be important. Sometimes, the author puts in clues, or details that seem as if they lead toward one person's guilt, that are proven wrong. (These false leads are called "red herrings.") Despite the frequent plot twists and turns, try to follow the sequence of events carefully. As the events unfold, the details become the clues that will help the hero solve the mystery. Remember, a good mystery remains puzzling until the end. So sit back, let suspense build, and get ready to be surprised!

Features of a Mystery

The plot revolves around solving a crime.

The detective reveals the culprit at the end of the story.

An amateur or professional detective is the main character.

The setting can be any time, any place.

The detective uses analytic skills to solve the crime.

The story may include a "red herring."

The detective uses previous knowledge to solve the crime.

There is a feeling of suspense throughout the story.

Who invented mysteries?

Early stories, such as the *Tales of the Arabian Nights*, had many plot twists. By the mid-1800s, Edgar Allan Poe added suspense and a character who used logical thinking to put clues together and solve crimes. By the late 1800s, the professional detective Sherlock Holmes, an invention of the writer Arthur Conan Doyle, used scientific methods and keen powers of observation to solve mysteries in Victorian England. Holmes's popularity led to dozens and dozens of other fictional detectives in the twentieth century.

Tools for Readers and Writers

Oxymoron

An oxymoron is a literary figure of speech usually made of two words that contradict, or oppose, each other. An oxymoron can be used for a dramatic effect as in *deafening silence* or *peace force*. It may also have a comical, or humorous, effect as in *jumbo shrimp*.

Authors include oxymorons as a way to make readers think about the text. When readers find an oxymoron, they should think about why the author chose to include it. Was the author being humorous, dramatic, or sarcastic, or was there some other intention?

Heterographs

Heterographs are words that are pronounced the same but are spelled differently and have different meanings. For example: *pear*, *pair*, and *pare*; *write*, *rite*, and *right*.

It is easy to make mistakes with heterographs, so it is important to read carefully and use context clues to know which one the author is using.

Make Inferences

Good authors don't explain everything in a story. Often, authors provide clues and evidence in their texts and expect the reader to "read between the lines," or make inferences. Good readers consider the information an author provides and think about other truths it suggests. To make an inference, look for parts of the text that makes you stop and think, *I wonder if the author is saying that . . .*

Meet the Characters

Samantha Snow, age fourteen, lives with her father Eubie in a small town near Philadelphia. Her mother died when she was in the fifth grade. Her braces finally came off and she's ecstatic about that. When not playing soccer or basketball, Sam has her pocket video camera out, or she's helping her dad in the garden center.

Sam's favorite thing to do is listen to music. But her dad thinks she's too young to go to concerts with her friends. He takes her instead. That would really annoy Sam, except that going to a concert with Eubie Snow means sitting in the VIP section, having laminated backstage passes, and meeting musicians!

It was at a concert, when she solved the problem of some mixed-up ticket stubs, that Sam first discovered she loved mysteries.

Eubie Snow retired from the music business thirty-plus years ago to pursue his dream of a quiet, country life, working at a garden center he started with his wife. Eubie had discovered and managed bands, many which went on to become superstars—years later. None of them ever forgot Eubie. That's why he still snags those perks.

Famous Fictional Youth Sleuths

Sam Snow joins a long line of fictional teen and kid sleuths, which is another word for *detective*. The best-loved include the following young detectives who, thanks to their personalities, adventures, and crime-solving abilities, still have millions of fans.

The Hardy Boys

Teenage brothers Frank and Joe have been solving mysteries in their hometown of Bayport since 1927. Detective work is in their blood: Their dad, Fenton, is a professional detective. The boys sometimes get involved in their dad's cases but are always involved in exciting adventures that lead to criminals being brought to justice.

Nancy Drew

Teenage Nancy Drew first burst onto the scene as an amateur detective in 1930. She quickly became known for her feisty and independent nature, as well as for her speedy blue car. Nancy solves crimes, either in her hometown of River Heights, where she lives with her lawyer father, or in more exotic places around the world. Nancy Drew was an unconventional female character back in the 1930s. Perhaps that's why she became an instant favorite among girls.

Edward Stratemeyer (1862–1930) created the Hardy Boys and Nancy Drew. His plucky teen detectives have appeared in hundreds of mystery books written by many different authors.

The Boxcar Children

The orphaned Alden kids—Henry, Jessie, Violet, and Benny, ages fourteen, twelve, ten, and six—live with their wealthy grandfather, who moves an abandoned boxcar into his backyard. The boxcar becomes a playhouse and headquarters for solving mysteries in the neighborhood. The Alden children also solve mysteries in places they visit with their grandfather.

Gertrude Chandler Warner (1890–1979) created the Boxcar Children. Her stories first appeared in the 1920s and were reprinted in the 1940s and 1950s. More recent books have been written by other authors.

Encyclopedia Brown

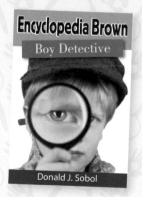

Ten-year-old Leroy "Encyclopedia" Brown has been a master at uncovering inconsistencies, unmasking pranksters, and solving mysteries in his hometown of Idaville since 1963. Working out of his "office" in the family garage on Rover Avenue, Encyclopedia takes on cases from neighborhood kids for twenty-five cents a day plus expenses. The series includes many short-story mysteries; readers are encouraged to use their own sleuthing skills to solve them.

Encyclopedia Brown was created and is written by Donald J. Sobol (1924–   ).

Whose Song Is It, Anyway?

S amantha Snow stopped cheering and fell into her seat. "Isn't Madame Olivia incredible?" she cried.

Her father feigned a grimly happy smile and shrugged. Eubie Snow liked the kind of music and musicians he used to represent thirty years ago, before he gave up the music business in favor of a quieter life. These days he rarely went to concerts, unless it was to accompany his fourteen-year-old daughter.

"No way!" he said every time she asked to go with her friends. "I know what happens at concerts!"

Sam didn't really mind being chaperoned by her dad, especially since he was still able to snag seats in the VIP section and get backstage passes for most events.

Madame Olivia returned to the stage for her encore. Sam jumped to her feet.

The keyboard player teased four notes, but no one was fooled. "This Conversation Is OVER!" was the number-one single on the pop charts, and everyone in the room recognized those notes. Madame Olivia took her **cue** from the keyboard player and began to sing.

Sam glanced down at her father and groaned. Eubie wasn't even watching the stage. He was talking to a tall, stately older woman seated to his left.

When the song ended and the house lights came on, Sam sat down and studied the crowd. People were starting to **queue** up for the usual end-of-concert forward retreat.

She wondered about the two women seated in front of her until she saw their laminated backstage passes. The last names on the passes were the same as Madame Olivia's.

Sam was eager to get backstage to meet Madame Olivia. She tried to get her father's attention.

"Of course I remember you, Rhonda," Eubie was saying. "How could I ever forget 'the lady with the velvet voice'?"

The woman laughed. "Eubie, you're too kind! I'm wondering if you can help me with something. Did you happen to recognize the melody of that last song, 'This Conversation Is OVER!'? Those first distinctive four notes? That's my tune, Eubie. I only sang it once, right here in this theater, thirty years ago, and it was never copyrighted. But I can prove it's mine, because luckily I made one tape of that song, and I just happen to have that old cassette right here in my purse."

Eubie pulled back and frowned at Sam as the woman reached under her seat to get her purse. It was clear that Eubie did not want to get involved.

"I don't think you've met my daughter," he said, quickly changing the subject. "Sam, this is Rhonda Redmond. I used to be her manager."

Sam's body tensed. So many things were happening at once. She was inches from Madame Olivia's family, who were getting ready to leave. And here was Rhonda Redmond accusing Sam's favorite singer of stealing her song.

Rhonda kept talking to Eubie even though it was obvious that he was uncomfortable. "I am planning to confront Madame Olivia with the tape," she said.

The older woman in front of them turned, smiled, and shook Rhonda's hand. "I couldn't help overhearing. I was a huge fan of yours. I have every single one of your records."

Rhonda blushed. Sam interrupted before she could get out "Thank you." "Are you related to Madame Olivia?" she asked the older woman.

"I'm her grandmother, and this is her mother. We live nearby, but it's our first visit to this beautiful old theater. We're so excited to be here."

Rhonda and Olivia's grandmother continued to chat, and Sam pulled Eubie aside. "Do you think there really is a tape?"

"Why wouldn't there be?" asked Eubie in reply.

"I don't know," said Sam. "It just seems odd that Rhonda would have a tape of a song she sang only once. Besides, Madame Olivia wasn't even born when Rhonda says she *did* sing that song. How could she have stolen it?"

Eubie shrugged. The crowd began to move, so he grabbed his blue **serge** jacket and followed Sam. They sidestepped the **surge** of the crowd and hesitated near the front of the stage.

"Where do we go now?" Eubie asked.

"I'm not sure," Olivia's mother said from behind them. "We haven't been backstage yet, so I'm afraid I don't know."

"If I remember correctly, it's that way." Rhonda pointed toward a maze of closed doors behind the stage.

Olivia's grandmother led the way, pushed open a gray steel door, and waited as the guard behind it examined her laminated pass. The others followed.

The little group made their way to the Meet and Greet room to wait for Madame Olivia. Rhonda placed her huge yellow leather purse on a table and started pulling things out: a small broken mirror, a flashlight, a notebook with papers spilling out, a pile of change, and a very old polka-dotted wallet.

"The tape's not here!" she shrieked as she dumped out the last bits and pieces. "Somebody stole it!"

"Maybe it was never there," Sam whispered to Eubie. "Maybe she's just trying to get some of Madame Olivia's royalties. Anyway, it's impossible to tell the date and time a cassette tape was recorded so it wouldn't really prove anything."

Rhonda stuffed her things back into her purse and sat in a chair by the wall. "It was definitely in my purse," she wailed. "I put it in there right before I left for the concert and I haven't opened my purse since."

Rhonda was crying now, and Sam was beginning to feel sorry for her. Maybe there really was a tape and somebody really had stolen it.

But when? If Rhonda was telling the truth, the tape must have been taken while they were watching Madame Olivia. Rhonda's purse was on the floor during the concert, but no one knew the tape was inside until after the concert, when Rhonda mentioned it.

Madame Olivia came in then, and Sam forgot all about Rhonda and the tape. She made her way through the gathering crowd and stood next to Sam. Sam was trying to think of the perfectly right thing to say when Rhonda Redmond angrily elbowed her way between them.

"You took my music!" Rhonda shouted at Madame Olivia. "The words are different, but those four notes and the rest of the melody are mine!"

The room grew quiet and then erupted into a cacophony of controlled chaos as everyone tried to speak at once. Sam backed away and leaned against the wall.

Sam needed to think. She was picturing the concert, and Rhonda's purse on the floor, and everyone who might have been close enough to get to it. There was the man next to Rhonda, the people in the row behind, and Madame Olivia's relatives.

Anyone could have taken that tape. Except . . . !

Eubie was standing next to Olivia's mother and grandmother when Sam joined them.

"I've been thinking," Sam said. "I've been thinking about doors, and opportunity, and little white lies. I've been thinking about someone who had the opportunity to take that tape out of Rhonda's purse and also told a lie. I've been thinking about a person who said she'd never been in this theater before but led us straight to the correct backstage door."

Sam stared at Olivia's grandmother. The elderly woman looked into Sam's eyes, set her jaw, then turned away.

"Grammy!" cried Madame Olivia.

"Have you also been thinking about motive?" said Olivia's grandmother with a sigh. "I love my granddaughter. When I heard Rhonda talking to Eubie, I panicked. I was afraid Olivia would get into trouble so I took the tape from Rhonda's purse and I lied. I *have* been in this theater before. But Olivia never stole that song. I guess I gave it to her."

"You gave it to her?" Eubie asked. "How?"

Olivia's grandmother was about to explain when Sam interrupted. "Allow me," she said. "You were at Rhonda's concert here thirty years ago, the one where she sang and taped her song. The tune stuck in your head, just like the melody of 'This Conversation Is OVER!' stuck in my head and everyone else's. You couldn't stop humming it, Olivia heard it when she was little, and it stuck in her head, too. Am I right?"

"Remarkable!" said Olivia's grandmother. "That's exactly what happened! So I guess, in a way, Olivia and I both really did take Rhonda's music—unintentionally."

It took Eubie several minutes to pull Madame Olivia away from Rhonda and the rest of the crowd, and quite a bit longer to explain about the melody and the tape. But when Olivia finally understood, she went straight to her grandmother and hugged her. Rhonda followed.

Olivia's grandmother opened her pocketbook and handed the tape to Rhonda. "I'm sorry," she said. "Really I am. I guess I got carried away."

Rhonda forgave her and slipped the tape back into her big yellow leather purse.

"I would never steal anyone's song on purpose," Madame Olivia said. "We'll work the money out, and maybe you can even join me onstage next week. We'll sing our song together. Would you like that?"

Rhonda Redmond smiled. Of course she would like that. She would like that very, very much.

Reread the Mystery

Analyze the Characters and Plot

- Who are the main characters in this mystery? Who are the minor characters?

- Why is Samantha's dad with her at the concert?

- Sam does not mind her father being with her at concerts. Why not?

- Why is Rhonda Redmond upset during the concert?

- Why is Rhonda Redmond upset after everyone goes backstage to see Olivia?

- How is the mystery solved?

- Who stole the tape?

Focus on Comprehension: Make Inferences

- Sam wonders about the two women in the seats in front of her until she sees their laminated backstage passes. What does she realize about them? What does Sam already know about backstage passes that helps her answer her question about the women?

- Sam is torn between someone her dad once knew and one of her favorite singers. How can you tell?

- Sam isn't sure she can trust Rhonda Redmond. How can you tell?

Focus on Protagonists

All stories have a protagonist, a main character who is the hero or heroine of the story.
- Who is the protagonist in this mystery?
- What positive character traits does the protagonist possess?

Analyze the Tools Writers Use: Oxymoron

- On page 8, the author says that Samantha's dad "feigned a grimly happy smile." *Grimly* and *happy* are opposites. What do you think this smile looked like?

- On page 9, the author says that people were gearing up "for the usual end-of-concert forward retreat." What did the author mean by this oxymoron?

- On page 13, the author says that the room erupted into "controlled chaos." How can chaos be controlled?

Focus on Words: Heterographs

Make a chart like the one below. Read each heterograph and identify its part of speech. Then identify the heterograph's definition. Finally, identify words from the text that helped you determine which heterograph the author used.

Page	Word	Part of Speech	Definition	Text Words That Helped You Choose the Correct Heterograph
9	cue			
9	queue			
11	serge			
11	surge			

The Mixed-Up Guitar Case

S am Snow was settling down in the third row of the auction house when the well-dressed man with the brilliant white hair tapped her father on the shoulder.

"Aren't you Eubie Snow?" the man asked in a booming voice.

Eubie glanced up, grinned, and jumped to his feet. "Raymond Maxwell!" Eubie said as he gave the man a big bear hug. "How long has it been?"

"It's been over thirty years since we both said our farewells to this crazy music business and went in search of a quieter life. I gave up the guitar, and you decided to quit managing crazy musicians like me. Are you still in the country, puttering around in your garden?"

"As much as I can be," Eubie laughed. "And I couldn't be happier."

"Me too," Raymond said. "I heard you donated that old guitar I gave you back then, so I thought I'd drop by for one last visit with it. That old 'axe' and I sure had some wild adventures. I'm glad I had a few minutes with it backstage."

The auctioneer banged his gavel and the two men took their seats.

"Ladies and gentlemen, welcome to the fifth annual Music in the Schools Auction. Please open your wallets, because all the money we raise today will be used to help children experience the magical world of music. Our first item is Raymond Maxwell's 1970 electric guitar. This is the one he used to record his big hit—"

"Only hit," Raymond whispered to Sam with a chuckle.

"—'Crazy Maisy.'"

Just then, a young man in a leather vest carried Raymond's old guitar out from the wings and played the opening riff of "Crazy Maisy." Then he carefully placed the guitar on the stand next to the podium.

"Thank you, Julian," the auctioneer said as the audience applauded politely. The young man stepped back.

Raymond poked Sam and pointed toward the stage. "That's my son, Julian, up there. He volunteered to help out at the auction. And, as you just heard, he's one good guitarist. If your father were still in the business, I'd be begging him to manage Julian."

The auctioneer pounded his gavel and called for order. The bidding began slowly and then picked up steam. At $4,000 the bidding slowed, and only two bidders remained.

"Do I hear five thousand?" the auctioneer called. A short man with long gray hair raised his hand. "Six thousand?" called the auctioneer.

"Six thousand!" shouted an excited middle-aged woman in a feathered hat sitting in the front row.

The author builds suspense with a bidding war for the guitar. She also introduces possible suspects. Could either of the people bidding be involved in the crime?

Raymond gasped. "I don't believe it," he whispered to Eubie, but loud enough for Sam to hear. "It's that wacko fan who used to follow me wherever I played. I'd recognize that voice anywhere. She was in the front row at every show, and boy, was she loud!"

Sam was only half-listening, studying the guitar. There was something about it, something she hadn't noticed before. She excused herself and moved along the wall to get a better look.

Sam knew Raymond Maxwell's guitar well. She had lived with it her whole life, and she had even played it a few times.

The guitar on the stage may have been a 1970 electric guitar, but it was definitely not the instrument Raymond Maxwell had given to her father. One of the strings was shiny and new! That morning, when Sam had carried the guitar into the auction house, every single string had been old and dull.

The guitar onstage was also missing a scratch and it had a bent tuning peg.

Raymond's obsessive fan and the little man with the long gray hair continued their bidding war.

The author introduces the mystery plot by having Sam, an amateur detective, realize that someone has switched guitars. Sam knows this because she has previous knowledge about the original guitar, having grown up with it in her house. She also uses her powers of observation to detect that one of the strings is new. This is a clue that something is wrong.

21

The woman was on her feet now, waving her arms wildly. "Eleven thousand, twelve thousand, thirteen thousand! I'll go higher, as high as it takes. I need that guitar!"

Sam returned to her seat and poked her father. "That's not the Maxwell guitar," she whispered. "I'm sure of it."

"What?" said Eubie, startled. "What are you talking about?"

"Just look at it," Sam urged her dad.

"Going once!" the auctioneer called. "Twice! Three times! Sold to the woman in the feathered hat for thirteen thousand dollars."

The woman jumped to her feet, waved her arms, and screeched.

"We've got to tell the auctioneer!" Sam told Eubie.

Sam pushed her way through the crowd and hurried onto the stage. Eubie whispered something to Raymond and the two quickly followed her.

When Sam finished talking to the auctioneer, she joined her dad, Raymond, and Raymond's son, Julian. Raymond introduced them to each other and Sam grabbed and shook Julian's hand.

Julian tried to pull free from Sam's grasp after several seconds, but Sam held firm. There was something she needed to find out before she let go. When she was done, she shook Raymond's hand, too.

The author has Sam use analytical skills when she shakes Julian's and then Raymond's hands. The detective is trying to find out something. What could it be? The reader plays along as an "armchair detective"—and tries to solve the mystery along with, or before, Sam.

"Excuse me for interrupting," the auctioneer said. "I need you all to come with me."

Sam, Eubie, Raymond, Julian, and the woman in the feathered hat followed the auctioneer to a small room in the back. The auctioneer placed the guitar with the shiny string on a stand in the middle of the room.

"I'm afraid we have a problem," he announced when they were settled. "Perhaps Sam will explain, since she spotted the switch."

The woman in the feathered hat was clearly confused. "What switch?" she cried.

Sam explained. "This isn't Raymond's old guitar. It's a genuine imitation. I brought the real guitar into this room myself, right before the auction started, and I'm guessing it's still here."

The woman fluttered her hands and squealed. "Oh, that's very good news. Can I have it now?"

"In a minute," Sam said, needing to stall a bit as she began to **canvass** the room. "Okay, let's begin with who was in here before the auction began."

"I was here," the auctioneer said. "And Julian, of course, before he carried the guitar to the stage."

"Yes, but there was one other person in this room before the auction started." Sam turned and faced Raymond. "Didn't you say you came backstage to see your guitar?"

Raymond's eyes grew wide and offended as he realized the implications of Sam's question.

"You loved that guitar," Sam continued.

"I did love it, but not enough to steal it," Raymond said angrily.

"Maybe," Sam muttered to herself as she glanced around the room. She was convinced that the Maxwell guitar was in there somewhere. But where?

The author continues to build suspense. Where is the real guitar?

A deafening silence settled in as everyone watched Sam explore the room, opening closets and cupboards, searching behind curtains and under coats. No one said a word. Everyone was waiting.

Then Sam spotted a guitar case on the closet shelf. It was a crowded **canvas** of rock and roll history. Every inch was covered with stickers with the names of bands: famous old bands, forgotten old bands, newer bands neither famous nor forgotten. Sam carried the case to the table, placed it beside the guitar with the shiny string, and opened it. "Is that my guitar?" the woman in the feathered hat asked.

Sam, the detective character, investigates.

Sam took the guitar from the case and studied it. "This is the real Maxwell guitar," she said as she handed it to the auctioneer.

"But whose case is it?" the auctioneer asked.

Raymond jumped to his feet. "It's mine," he announced, in that booming voice. "I'm so sorry, but when I saw my old guitar again I couldn't resist, and I switched them before the auction. I'd missed it too much."

"That's not your case," Sam said quickly.

"Of course it is!" protested Raymond.

Sam took an open packet from the case, pulled out the strings that were inside, and held them next to the shiny string on the guitar that *wasn't* the Maxwell. They matched perfectly.

"These don't belong to you, Raymond," she said. "You haven't played the guitar in years. But Julian has."

"That's ridiculous." Raymond's voice was softer now, and his face wore an expression of sweet sorrow. Julian stood and took the strings from Sam. "They're mine, all right," he said quietly. "I didn't mean to be **callous** or uncaring. I switched the guitars because I knew how much my dad loved that old guitar and I wanted him to have it. Dad was just protecting me."

"That's what I thought," Sam said gently.

Raymond put his arms around his son and held him close. After a minute, he let go and asked Sam how she had figured out it was Julian who switched the guitars.

"Your son's fingertips gave him away," she explained. "Each one has a **callus**. Just to make sure, I felt your fingertips, too, when I shook your hand. People who play the guitar build up calluses on their fingertips. Julian's are hard, which means he probably breaks a lot of strings. Your fingertips are soft, Raymond, because you haven't played for a long time."

Julian looked at the floor. "I'm so sorry. I guess I didn't stop to think I was actually stealing something," he said to the room. "What happens now?"

The author has Sam use previous knowledge (about guitar-players' calluses) and put together the clues to solve the crime. Sam, the detective, reveals that Julian was the culprit who switched the guitars.

Everyone knew that Julian had just meant to do something nice for his father. Nobody wanted to call the police. The auctioneer had to go back to the auction, and the woman in the feathered hat was so delighted to have her guitar that she didn't care what happened next.

Sam and Eubie had a quick and quiet conversation in a corner. Then Eubie said, "Julian, we figure that even if no one presses charges, you should still do something to balance this out."

"Anything!" Julian agreed, relieved.

"How about a Raymond and Julian Maxwell Benefit Concert for Music in the Schools?" Sam suggested.

"Yes, yes, yes!" Julian and Raymond both agreed at once.

The author shows the characters' personalities in this exchange of dialogue: Julian really meant no harm and everyone wants to help make things right. Sam, the hero, comes up with a way to do this.

Raymond's fan screamed, "Yes! And you can even use your old guitar! I'll lend it to you!"

Raymond smiled and said, "And I have a surefire way to make sure no one ever mixes up guitars again." And with that he autographed his Maxwell. His fan squealed louder than ever.

Analyze the Characters and Plot

- Who are the main characters in this mystery? Who are the minor characters?

- What is the setting of the mystery?

- What is Eubie auctioning?

- What does Sam realize about the guitar that was onstage? How does she figure out that something is wrong?

- How is the mystery solved?

- Who switched the guitar?

Focus on Comprehension: Make Inferences

- Eubie and Raymond haven't seen each other in years. How can you tell that their appearances changed over time?

- Eubie and Raymond Maxwell have a good relationship. How can you tell?

- What can you tell about the two people who are in a bidding war for the guitar?

- The guitar case is very special. How can you tell?

Analyze the Tools Writers Use: Oxymoron

- On page 23, the author says that the guitar onstage isn't Raymond's old guitar. It's a "genuine imitation." *Genuine* and *imitation* are opposites. What does the author mean by saying this?

- On page 24, the author says that a "deafening silence settled in." How can silence be deafening? In what circumstances would silence be deafening?

- On page 26, the author says that Raymond "wore an expression of sweet sorrow." How can sorrow be sweet? What might this expression look like?

Focus on Words: Heterographs

Make a chart like the one below. Read each heterograph and identify its part of speech. Then identify the heterograph's definition. Finally, identify words from the text that helped you determine which heterograph the author used.

Page	Word	Part of Speech	Definition	Text Words That Helped You Choose the Correct Heterograph
24	canvass			
24	canvas			
26	callous			
26	callus			

How does an author write a

Mystery?

Reread "The Mixed-Up Guitar Case" and think about what Dina Anastasio did to write this mystery. How did she develop the story? How can you, as a writer, develop your own mystery?

1. Decide on a Detective

Fictional detectives come in all shapes, sizes, ages, and types, from spunky kids to nosy old ladies to tough-talking ex-cops. You can write an original story based on the personality traits of a fictional detective created by another author, or you can invent your own supersleuth. For more information on Sam Snow and other fictional youth sleuths, see pages 5–7.

Mystery writers ask these questions:

- What kind of person is my detective? What does he or she like? Dislike?
- What is important to my detective?
- Will my detective character have an assistant? What is that person's relationship to the detective?
- What is that character's traits? Interests?

2. Brainstorm Other Characters

- What other characters will be in my story?
- Which characters will be suspects? How?

3. Brainstorm Setting and Plot

- Where does my mystery take place? When does it take place? How will I describe the place and time?
- What is the mystery that needs to be solved?
- Who are the main suspects?
- Will I include a "red herring"? If so, what?

Brainstorm Clues

Mystery writers include clues throughout their stories. Ask yourself, *What clues will I include?*

Detective Skills

Mystery writers include opportunities for the story's detective to show off detective skills. How will I include the skills of observing what happens, interviewing witnesses, and using what the detective already knows?

Detective	Samantha Snow
Assistant	Eubie Snow
Setting	an auction house in Philadelphia
Mystery	A guitar belonging to a one-time rock star has been replaced with a fake.
Clues	1. The guitar up for auction looks different than the one Sam and Eubie brought to the auction. 2. The guitar onstage has one shiny string. The real one had no shiny strings. 3. The guitar onstage is missing a scratch that the original one had and has one bent tuning peg.
Detective Skills	1. Sam uses observation skills and previous knowledge to determine that the auctioned guitar is not the real one. 2. Sam uses analytical skills to figure out that someone must have broken a string while playing the guitar and replaced it with a shiny new string. 3. Sam shakes hands with Julian and Raymond to feel for hard calluses, which could cause a string to break. 4. Sam realizes that the real guitar must still be backstage and finds it in an old guitar case.
Solution	Julian is the thief. Sam uses her previous knowledge that guitarists get calluses on their fingers from playing. Raymond hadn't played the guitar in years. Sam confirms this for herself when she shakes Raymond's hand and feels no calluses. Julian, who currently plays the guitar, has calluses on his fingers.

Glossary

callous   (KA-lus) insensitive (page 26)

callus   (KA-lus) thickened or hardened skin, often on the fingers, that has been subjected to a lot of friction (page 26)

canvas   (KAN-vus) strong cloth on which artists draw (page 24)

canvass   (KAN-vus) to walk and look around (page 24)

cue   (KYOO) a signal (page 9)

queue   (KYOO) to line up (page 9)

serge   (SERJ) a wool fabric used in clothing (page 11)

surge   (SERJ) sudden powerful forward movement (page 11)